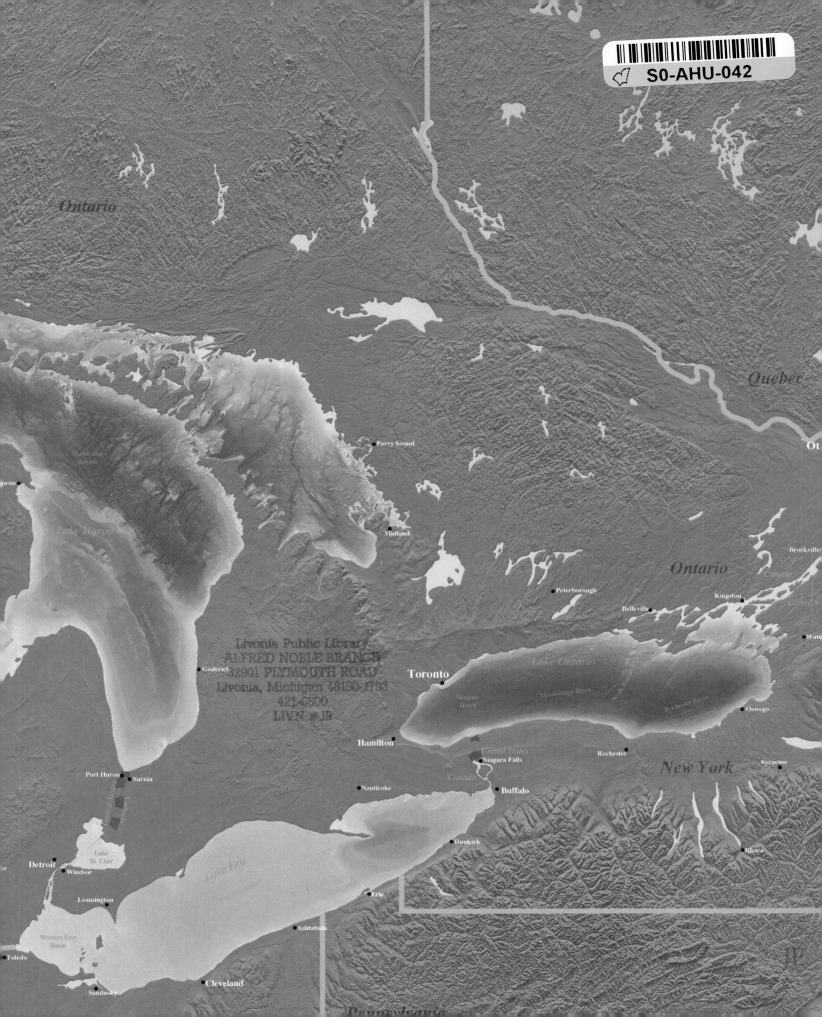

Ontario

Quebec

Ot

Parry Sound

Midland

Brockville

Ontario

Peterborough

Kingston

Belleville

Canada

United S

Lake Huron

Goderich

Lake Ontario

Niagara
Basin

Mississauga Basin

South Shore

Rochester Basin

Wate

Toronto

Oswego

Hamilton

Rochester

New York

Syracuse

United States

Niagara Falls

Canada

Nanticoke

Buffalo

Port Huron

Sarnia

Dunkirk

Ithaca

Detroit

Lake
St. Clair

Windsor

Lake Erie

Leamington

Erie

Western Erie
Basin

Ashtabula

Toledo

Cleveland

Sandusky

Pennsylvania

IV

THE DAY
THE GREAT LAKES
DRAINED AWAY

Written and Illustrated by Charles Ferguson Barker

Mackinac Island Press

For Peg,
and everyone who
loves the Great Lakes.

Thanks to the NOAA/National Geophysical Data Center

World Data Center for Marine Geology and Geophysics, Boulder, CO

for the bathymetry maps used on the inside cover of this book.

http://www.ngdc.noaa.gov/mgg/greatlakes/greatlakes.html

First Edition
Library of Congress Cataloging-in-Publication Data

Barker, Charles Ferguson
The Day the Great Lakes Drained Away
Summary: Explore what would happen if all of the water drained from the Great Lakes
and what their lake floors might look like under all that water.

ISBN 0-9749145-2-5
Fiction
10 9 8 7 6 5 4 3 2 1
Printed and bound in Canada by Friesens, Altona, Manitoba
A Mackinac Island Press, Inc. publication

Foreword

From the 19th century poet Henry Wadsworth Longfellow to 20th century author Ernest Hemingway, the grandeur of the Great Lakes has never ceased to inspire or fuel the imaginations of any and all who cast their gaze upon their endless blue horizons.

And that inspiration and fascination continues into the 21st century. Thanks to the Great Lakes' astronaut Jerry Linenger—a Michigan native—he could peer down from his small porthole aboard the Mir space station and pick out his home on the globe below. "Michigan's Lower Peninsula," he said, "does, indeed, appear to have been formed by a giant who, with a mitten on his hand, pushed down on that section of the planet."

Carved out by a massive retreating glacier more than 12,000 years ago, the Great Lakes have not only helped shape the history of Michigan and the United States, they have also helped define our unique character and culture.

A culture whose roots go back to the area's very first residents—the Native Americans—and the adventurous explorers and sea captains who braved the unpredictability of the Lakes in search of the next new frontier. It is a culture that has come to revere and respect the beauty and vulnerability of these most precious of all natural resources.

It is my sincere wish that you and your children and your children's children continue to be filled with that same sense of reverence and respect, and that they be instilled with a sense of pride and commitment to protecting these rare and irreplaceable resources—the greatest of all lakes— the Great Lakes.

Governor Jennifer M. Granholm

The Great Lakes were flowing with water
on every Great Lakes Day;
Until something frightful happened
and made the Great Lakes drain away.

Some thought it might have been an earthquake.
Some say it might have been a big pipe.
But whatever was draining the Great Lakes
it just didn't seem quite right.

Was there not enough rain this year?
Was the sun too hot?
Some people think not!

When the Great Lakes began to drain,
the lake levels dropped only a few inches a year;
So no one thought much about it…
it seemed there was nothing to fear.

eople would borrow just a little water, from their "just a little pipe."
hey thought it didn't matter. They said, "the Great Lakes will be all right!"

oon many people were borrowing water from the Great Lakes,
eir "one small pipe" became thousands...

ith the Great Lakes water at stake.

As water levels continued to drop, the people who noticed the most,
were people who had boats on the lakes,
and those who lived by the coast.

Soon the water from the Great Lakes would drain low,
until it was almost gone.
Fear around the Great Lakes was strong!

Lake Ontario's water level fell so low…OH NO!

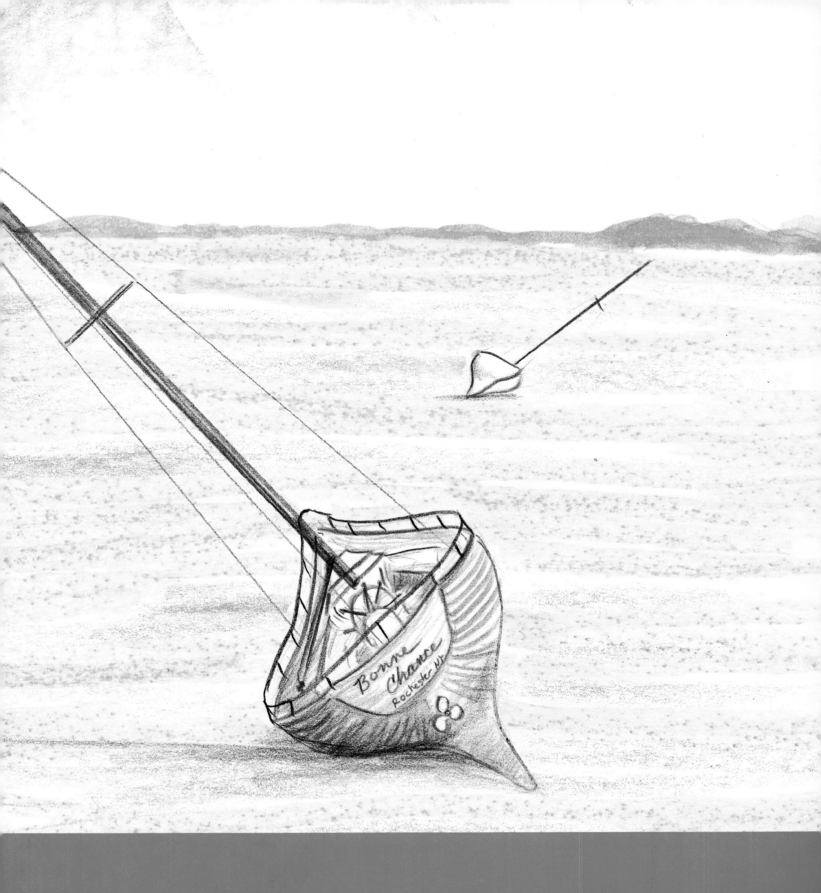

You could wade, instead of sail, from Rochester to Toronto.

Now, on the east side of Lake Ontario's floor
you could walk right up to a big old meteor crater...
it was bigger than a Great Lakes freighter.

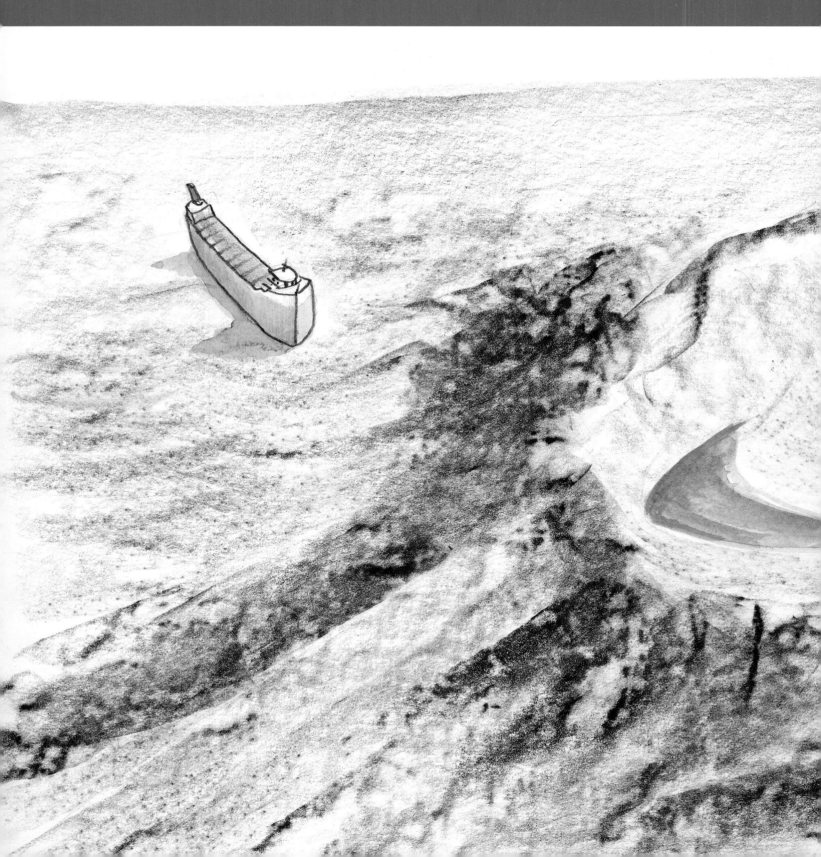

It was like something you would see on the moon.
Let's hope another one doesn't hit anytime soon!

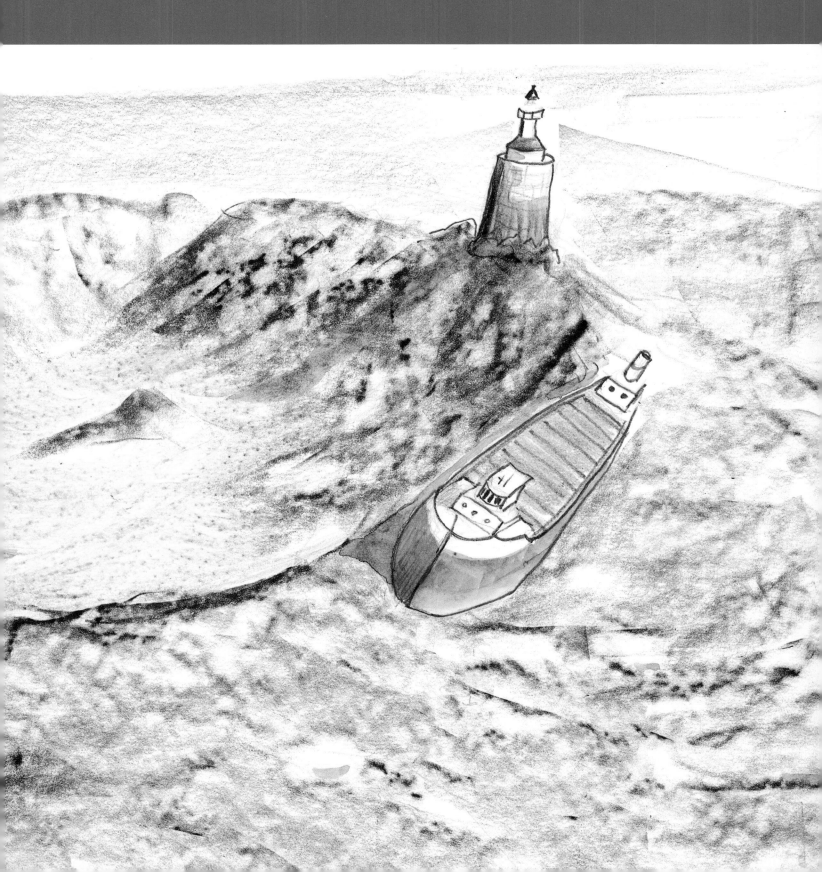

The mighty Niagara Falls had gone from rushing water to just a little trickle.
The town's hotels and shops found themselves in quite a big pickle...
NO ONE WOULD COME!

The town even renamed the famous boat they loved, "Maid of the Mist," to the "Maid of the Mud."
Still...NO ONE WOULD COME!

Lake Erie drained out muddy and flat.

You could even walk to Pelee Island from Cleveland and back.

The Detroit River drained away and totally stopped.

The freighters were stuck in the mud and you could walk up to their big metal props.

Now from Detroit to Windsor,
no need to use the tunnel or bridge.

Just drive across the dried up riverbed,
along the gravel ridge.

Lake St. Clair drained out flat and muddy too...
but there were lots of interesting artifacts on the bottom to view.
Some were really old; others were quite new.
Can we name a few?

A sunken yacht,
an old birch-bark canoe,
a mysterious wooden box,
and even an old shoe.

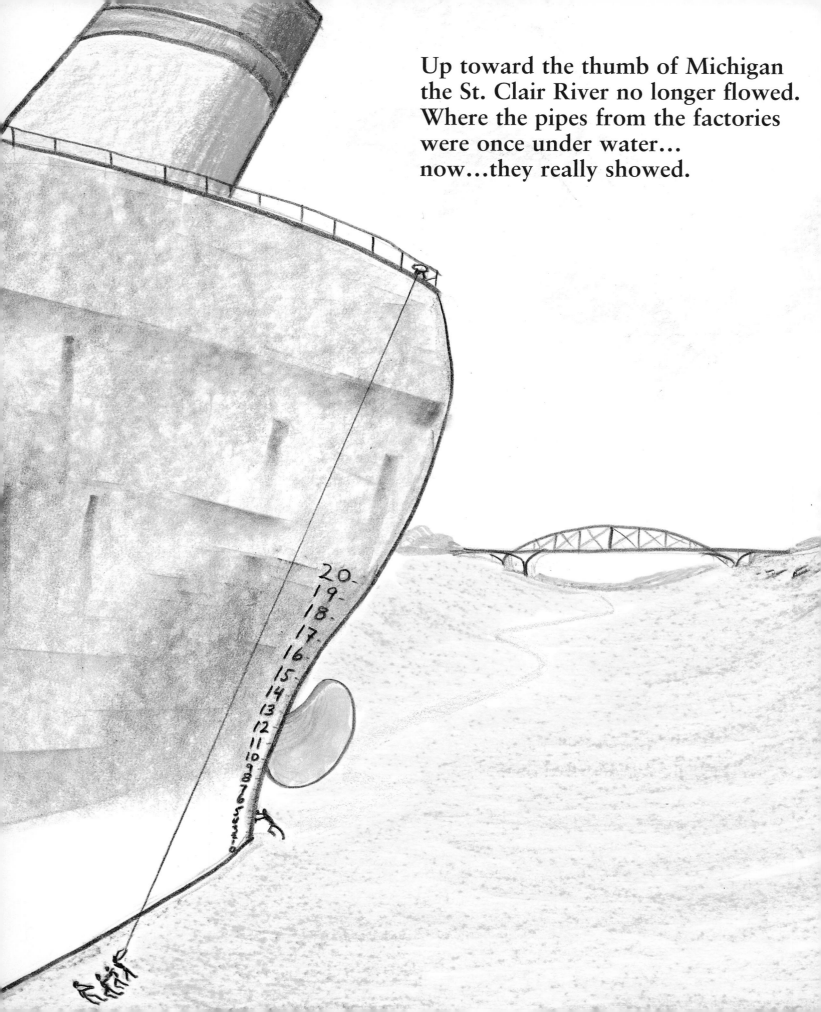

Up toward the thumb of Michigan
the St. Clair River no longer flowed.
Where the pipes from the factories
were once under water...
now...they really showed.

4

When Lake Huron drained away,
the sights to see were incredible.
There were huge tall ridges of rock to
climb, right smack dab in the middle!

In the deepest parts of the
drained away lakes,
there were caves the size of houses…
some were even bigger!
They were carved out where the
limestone rock had dissolved
away like sugar.

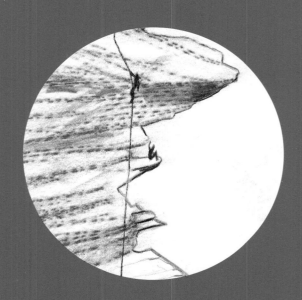

In the drained out Straits of Mackinac,
the Islands became big humps
in the lake floor.
They looked like castles with moats.
You could walk to Mackinac Island,
but it wasn't nearly as much fun
as riding the ferryboats.

When Lake Michigan drained away,
the muddy bottom dried up as hard as plaster.
At least it made the drive between
Michigan and Wisconsin much faster!

Barrels and barrels appeared all over the lake floor.
Bright orange and stuck in the sand,
they were covered with zebra mussels galore.

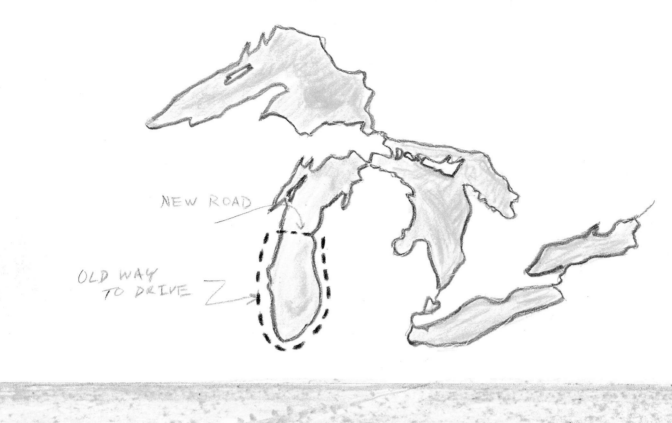

NEW ROAD

OLD WAY
TO DRIVE

FLOOR
LAKE SHORE DRIVE

NO DUMPING

All of the bays drained away...not a trickle...not a splash!
You could see all of the shipwrecks at the famous Manitou Pass.

On the bottom of Lake Huron lived a lost forest.
It lived during the times of the glaciers. How old is it? Can you guess?

It's been hiding under Lake Huron for thousands of years,
until the Great Lakes drained away and made it appear!

Way up north, the St. Mary's River
from Lake Superior was a dried up riverbed, too.

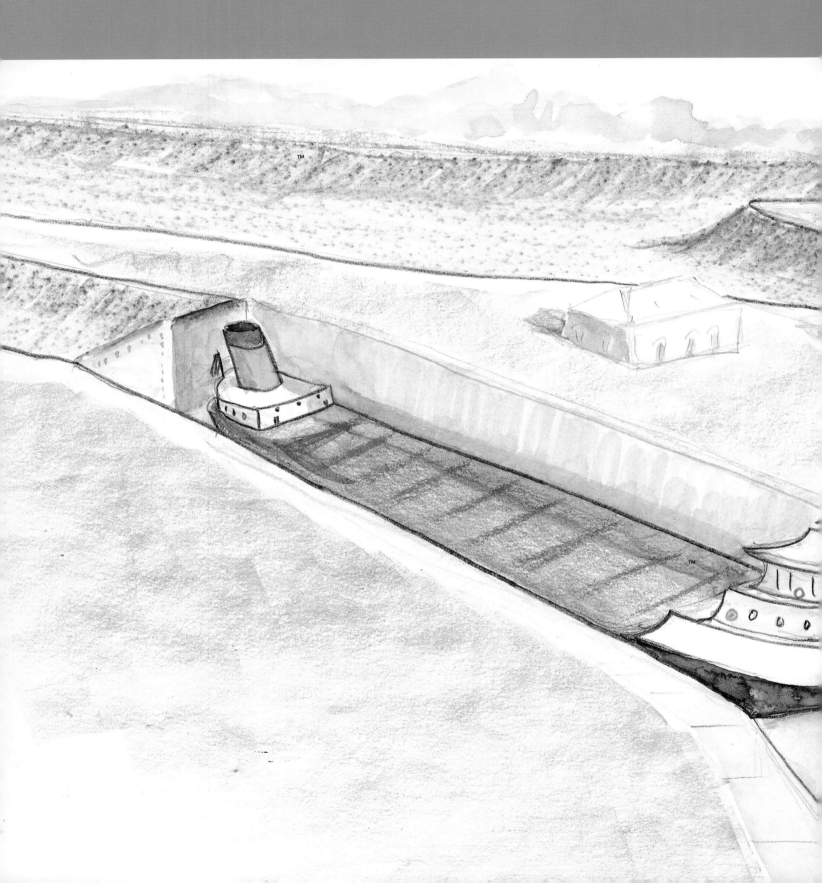

So they decided to turn the Soo Locks into a big swimming pool...
And named it...THE SOO!

Lake Superior was drained way down to the bottom,
over a thousand feet deep.
There were big heavy chunks of copper and gold...
you could drag out to keep.

Almost everyone was shocked when the
Great Lakes were all drained away and empty.
But there were interesting things on the
lake floors...and trust me...
THERE WERE PLENTY!

You could find anchors, and ship's wheels,
lost golden rings, and lots of other once-sunken things.

With all the water gone you could fish with ease.
Just walk out onto the lake floor and pick up as many as you please.
Soon that wasn't as much fun as you might think,
with all those stranded fish, it really began to stink!

With the water drained away it was getting quite grim.
No water for a boat ride, or even a Great Lakes swim.
Even then some people didn't care,
until the city water supply intakes
started sucking in air.

People never thought about
where their water had come from.
They had always just turned on the faucet,
AND SWOOSH, OUT IT WOULD COME!

Many Great Lakes cities draw water from the Lakes.
Does the city you live in have a Great Lakes intake?

Chicago, Duluth and even Milwaukee,
Ontonagon, Marquette and Sault St. Marie.

St. Ignace, Traverse City, Alpena,
Port Huron, Windsor and Sarnia.

Bay City, Detroit, Cleveland and Buffalo.
Think that's all? HEAVENS NO!

There's Rochester, Toronto and Evanston,
And the list goes on and on!

Sheboygan, Manitowoc…I'm sure we've missed a few,
like the hundreds of smaller Great Lakes' towns, too!

So now everyone missed the water
and all of the fun things to do.
There was no vacationing on the Great Lakes…
because that all dried up, too.

Now all the people who borrowed just a little water
from their "just a little pipe"
soon realized the Great Lakes were not all right.

So the people stopped taking water from the lakes
with their "just a little pipe."
And day by day the lakes filled back up,
making them once again a beautiful sight!

Now the Great Lakes are flowing
with water once again,
so deep and fresh and blue.
We must treat them as a treasure,
as a gift our whole lives through.

So…in the end…
what drained the Great Lakes away
wasn't an earthquake.
It wasn't a big pipe.
It wasn't one single lone villain.

It was….everyone's "just one small pipe"…
TIMES A MILLION!

Author's Note

The inspiration for this book was a result of seeing the tremendous maps of the underwater features (bathymetry) of the Great Lakes from the National Geophysical Data Center in Boulder, Colorado. One of these maps is shown on the inside cover of this book and others can be viewed on their website at www.ngdc.noaa.gov (look for Bathymetry-Great Lakes). These maps show the fascinating landscape that lies hidden beneath the Great Lakes.

My goal was to present these amazing lake floor features in a children's book with illustrations based on the actual bathymetry (although exaggerated for impact). The Great Lakes needed to have been drained away, but how? Easy enough to do with pencil and paper!

Although I originally set out to simply show the interesting landscape at the bottom of the Great Lakes, the topic inevitably brings up the vitally important issue of withdrawal and/or diversions of water from the Great Lakes by humans. Rather than avoid that controversial subject by bringing in aliens from outer space to drain the lakes away, the story evolved with the ideas and input of the talented writer Anne Margaret Lewis. Anne's words and suggestions helped make the story more interesting and fun to read.

Are the Great Lakes really likely to drain as in the story by "all those little pipes?" No, they are not. Is it worth considering (however fanciful) so we may never take the Great Lakes for granted? Absolutely!

The Great Lakes, geologically speaking, are a fleeting condition just as the warm tropical seas and sandy beaches that covered the area millions of years ago were (though they are welcome to return every mid-winter by most Great Lakes region residents). So, whether ultimately the Great Lakes are to evaporate, fill with sediment, expand and cover the region, or be drained away by a pipe or an earthquake, we can still appreciate and respect them while they are here. We are lucky to have them—imagine for a moment if they were gone.

GREAT LAKES FACTS

	Superior	Michigan	Erie	Huron	Ontario
Length	350 mi (563 km)	307 mi (494 km)	241 mi (388 km)	206 mi (332 km)	193 mi (311 km)
Breadth	160 mi (257 km)	118 mi (190 km)	57 mi (92 km)	183 mi (245 km)	53 mi (85 km)
Average depth	483 ft (147 m)	279 ft (85 m)	62 ft (19 m)	195 ft (59 m)	283 ft (86 m)
Maximum depth	1,332 ft (406 m)	925 ft (282 m)	210 ft (64 m)	750 ft (229 m)	802 ft (244 m)
Volume	2,900 mi^3 (12,100 km^3 or 12,100,000,000, 000,000 liters)	1,180 mi^3 (4,920 km^3 or 4,920,000,000, 000,000 liters)	116 mi^3 (484 km^3 or 484,000,000, 000,000 liters)	850 mi^3 (3,540 km^3 or 3,540,000,000, 000,000 liters)	393 mi^3 (1,640 km^3 or 1,640,000,000, 000,000 liters)
Water surface area	31,700 mi^2 (82,100 km^2)	22,300 mi^2 (57,800 km^2)	9,910 mi^2 (25,700 km^2)	23,000 mi^2 (59,600 km^2)	7,340 mi^2 (18,960 km^2)
Drainage basin area	49,300 mi^2 (127,700 km^2)	45,600 mi^2 (118,000 km^2)	30,140 mi^2 (78,000 km^2)	51,700 mi^2 (134,100 km^2)	24,720 mi^2 (64,030 km^2)
Shoreline length*	2,726 mi (4,385 km)	1,638 mi (2,633 km)	871 mi (1,402 km)	3,827 mi (6,157 km)	712 mi (1,146 km)
Elevation	600 ft (183 m)	577 ft (176 m)	569 ft (173 m)	577 ft (176 m)	243 ft (74 m)
Outlet	St. Marys River to Lake Huron	Straits of Mackinac to Lake Huron	Niagara River and Welland Canal	St. Clair River to Lake Erie	St. Lawrence River to the Atlantic Ocean
Replacement time**	191 years	99 years	2.6 years	22 years	6 years

* = including islands
** = the amount of time it takes nature to replace all of the water in the lake

WHERE DO YOU LIVE?

Image courtesy of the Great Lakes Information Network (GLIN).

For more information on the Great Lakes go to: www.great-lakes.net/teach/geog/intro/intro_2.html

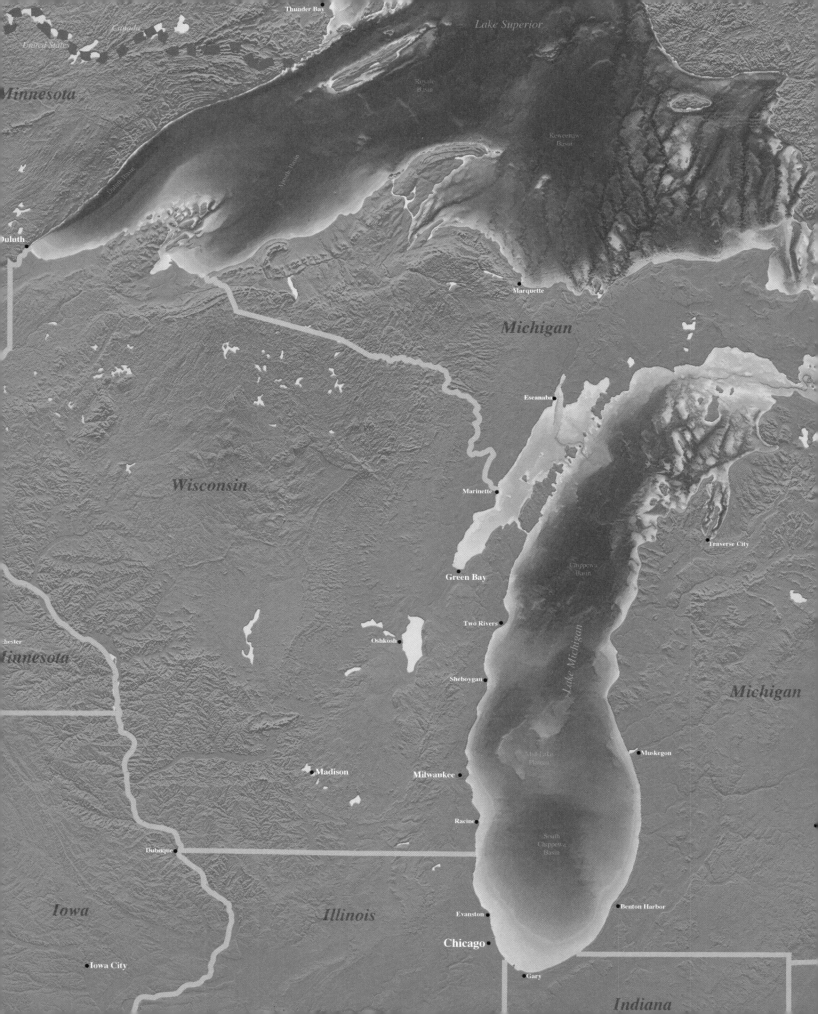